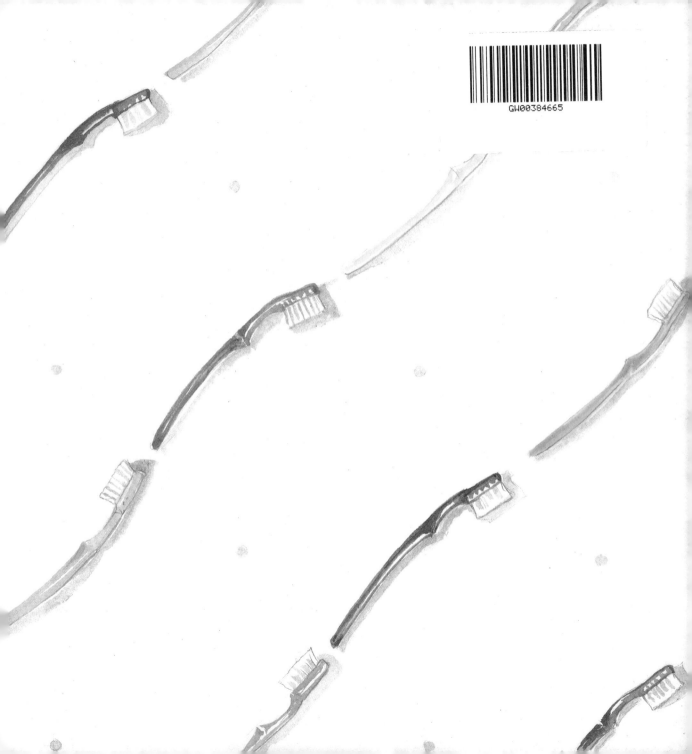

GW00384665

For Renate,
who made Bertie

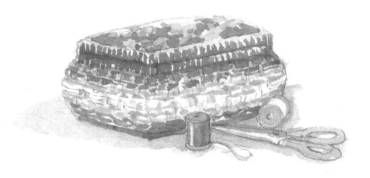

British Library Cataloguing in Publication Data
Bouma, Paddy
Bertie at the dentist's.
I. Title
823[J]   PZ7
ISBN 0-370-31045-4

Copyright © Paddy Bouma 1987
Photoset by Rowland Phototypesetting Ltd
Bury St Edmunds, Suffolk
Printed in Great Britain for
The Bodley Head Ltd
32 Bedford Square, London WC1B 3EL
by W. S. Cowell Ltd,
Ipswich, Suffolk
First published 1987

Bertie
at the Dentist's

Paddy Bouma

The Bodley Head
London

Bertie was Thomas's toy hippo. They went everywhere together. On the day that Thomas had to go to the dentist's for a check-up, he took Bertie along.

"Hop up here, Thomas," said the
dentist.
"Let's take a look."

Thomas climbed on to the dentist's chair. Bertie sat on his tummy and watched. The chair sank back. Then it shot up into the air. Bertie nearly fell off.

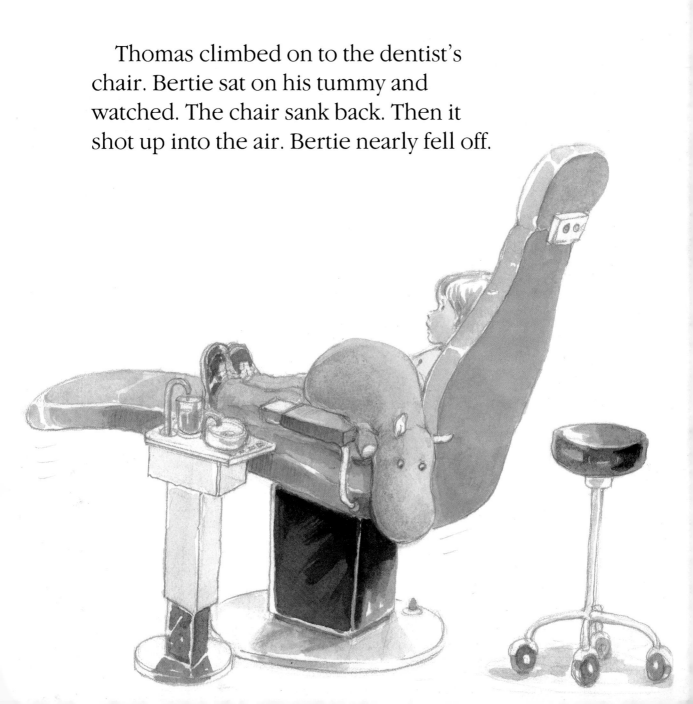

"You sit here, Bertie," said the dentist. He began to wash his hands.

Bertie was fascinated. He had never seen soap in a bottle before.

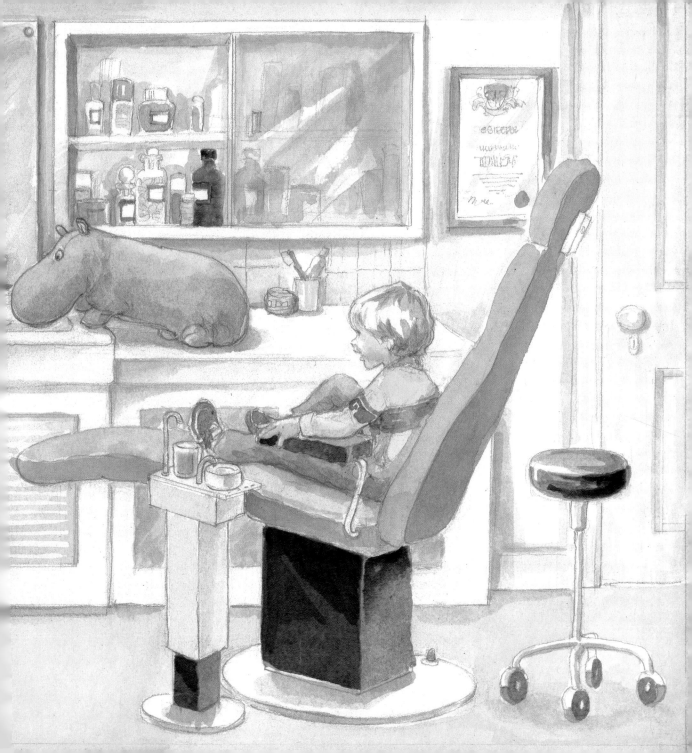

When the dentist was not looking,
Bertie wrote a big "B" on the mirror
with the soap.

Thomas frowned at him.

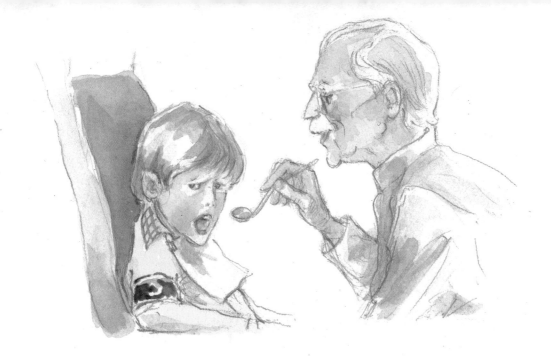

The dentist began examining
Thomas's teeth with a little mirror.
　　Bertie spotted an enormous pair of
dentures. They looked as if they might
fit . . . THEY DID!
　　Thomas glared at him.

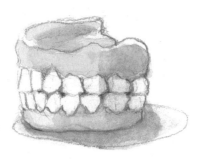

"You should always brush your teeth thoroughly," the dentist told Thomas.

Bertie came upon a large toothbrush and some toothpaste. In no time he had brushed up a glorious foam. Thomas squirmed in his chair.

The dentist pulled out some dental
floss to clean between Thomas's teeth.
Bertie watched, entranced. He liked
the way it came out of the container, but
it was some time before he discovered
how to cut it off.

Thomas made frantic signs at him
from behind the dentist's back.

"You should not eat too many
sweets," said the dentist. Bertie found
some sugar-free gum in the cupboard.
He blew a large bubble.

Thomas closed his eyes, braced
himself and waited . . .

"What was that?" said the dentist.
Luckily he had the wrong specs on and
couldn't see Bertie cleaning the gum off
his nose.

"No cavities, young man. You can get down. Don't forget Bertie," said the dentist.

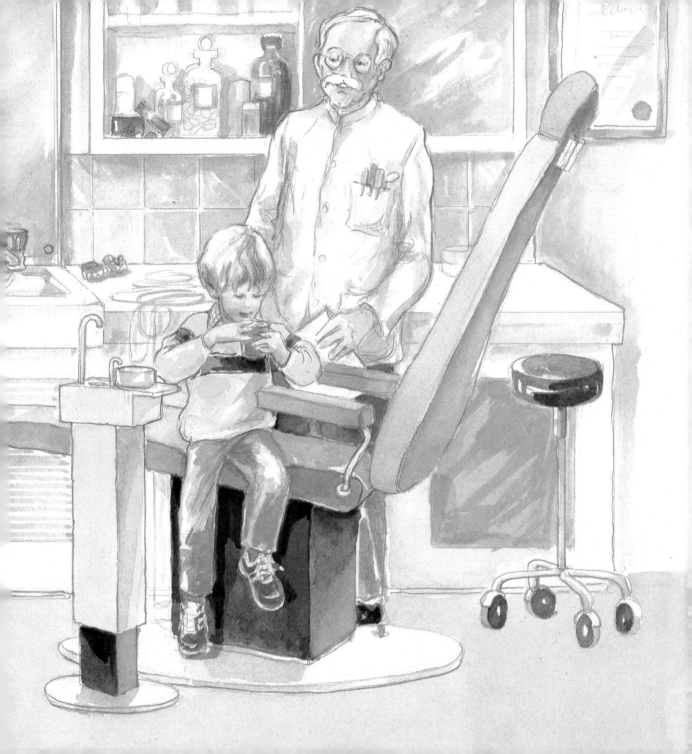

Thomas left in a hurry.

His little sister, Tessa, was waiting for him.

"Were you scared?" she asked.

"No I wasn't," said Thomas. "And nor was Bertie!"

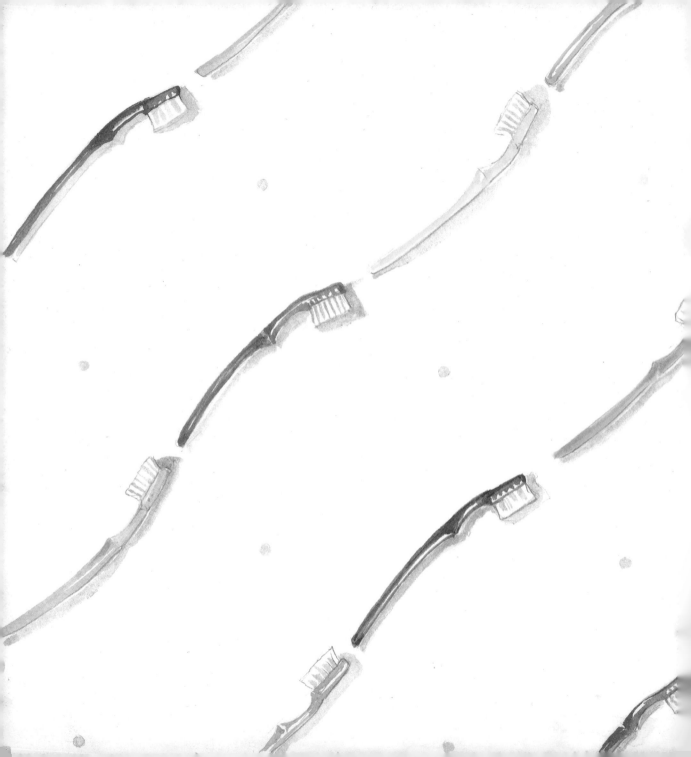